The Weird Sisters

A Robin, a Ribbon, and a Lawn Mower

Owlkids Books acknowledges the financial support of the Canada Council for the Arts, the Ontario Arts Council, the Government of Canada through the Canada Book Fund (CBF) and the Government of Ontario through the Ontario Creates Book Initiative for our publishing activities.

Owlkids Books gratefully acknowledges that our office in Toronto is located on the traditional territory of many nations, including the Mississaugas of the Credit, the Chippewa, the Wendat, the Anishinaabeg, and the Haudenosaunee Peoples.

Published in Canada by Owlkids Books Inc., 1 Eglinton Avenue East, Toronto, ON M4P 3A1
Published in the US by Owlkids Books Inc., 1700 Fourth Street, Berkeley, CA 94710

Library of Congress Control Number: 2022938994

LIBRARY AND ARCHIVES CANADA CATALOGUING IN PUBLICATION

Title: The weird sisters : a robin, a ribbon, and a lawn mower / Mark David Smith ; illustrations by Kari Rust.
Other titles: Robin, a ribbon, and a lawn mower
Names: Smith, Mark David, 1972- author. | Rust, Kari, illustrator.
Description: Series statement: Weird Sisters Detective Agency; 2
Identifiers: Canadiana 20220252351 | ISBN 9781771474597 (hardcover)
Classification: LCC PS8637.M56524 W47 2023 | DDC jC813/.6—dc23

Edited by Katherine Dearlove | Designed by Elisa Gutiérrez

Manufactured in Guangdong Province, Dongguan City, China, in September 2022, by Toppan Leefung Packaging & Printing (Dongguan) Co., Ltd. Job #BAYDC114

A   B   C   D   E   F

Mark David Smith

The Weird Sisters

A Robin, a Ribbon, and a Lawn Mower

Illustrations by Kari Rust

OWLKIDS BOOKS

For Don Krause, mentor and friend —M.D.S.

For Margaret and Barry —K.R.

Contents

Summer Blues

When the people of Covenly had a mystery to solve, they never hired the members of The Three Sisters' Detective Agency: not Hildegurp, not Yuckmina, not Glubbifer. The sisters were *too* weird. One was bony, one was round, and one had knuckles that rubbed the ground.

They had brooms but never swept. They owned no car but never missed an event.

They ran their pet emporium and detective agency from the bottom floor of their home at

1313 Jitters Drive, which overlooked the town.
The house suited the sisters and their cat,

Graymalkin, perfectly. It wasn't a scary house at all.

If you were a spider.

Or a ghoul.

People, however, stayed away. All except their young friend, Jessica Nibley.

"We have no business!" Hildegurp complained while the sisters and Jessica walked the pets. "No one comes to our pet emporium."

"Or asks us to solve a mystery," added Yuckmina.

Graymalkin seemed to dislike her harness.

"Harumph," Glubbifer grumped, scooping the cat up into her coat. Glubbifer always expressed herself in as few words as possible.

"I'm blue too," Jessica said.

"People are not blue, Jessica Nibley," Hildegurp said.

"I could turn you into a frog," Yuckmina offered. "Then you would be green."

"No," Jessica explained, "*blue* means sad. I'm blue because school's out and I have no projects, and you're blue because you have no business."

"People think the three of us are too weird." Hildegurp sighed. "How can we fit in?"

"I'm not sure," Jessica said. "Some people like using the tire swing. I could teach you. It'll cheer us up at least."

"Are you sure?" Hildegurp asked.

"It's easy," Jessica insisted. "You just pump your legs."

"We do not pump legs, Jessica Nibley," Yuckmina explained. "Legs are not flat tires."

"*Pump* means push your legs out, then pull them back in. That's how you make the swing move."

"Exhausting," said Yuckmina. "I see why it is called a *tire* swing."

"No," said Jessica, "it's fun! You'll feel like you're flying."

Glubbifer clapped her hands.

"We like flying," Hildegurp said.

CHAPTER 2

Cosmo Has a Secret

O n their way to Covenly's only swing, they paused at Cosmo Keene's house. His lawn was overgrown and dotted with wildflowers. This was unlike him. He often said that only trouble-makers let their lawns grow wild. Jessica's goat strained to nibble a purple flower.

"Pansies!" Yuckmina said. "We will help by picking these from Cosmo's lawn."

Glubbifer yanked out a handful.

"Out of the way!" Cosmo barked, stepping from a large truck parked on the street. "Or my

dolly might run you over." On his dolly was a large, heavy box.

"Cosmo Keene," Hildegurp asserted, "*that* is a box. Dollies are small toys for kids." Glubbifer wagged a finger and shook her head at Hildegurp. "Oops! I mean, dollies are toys for *children*, not for baby goats," Hildegurp corrected. Glubbifer nodded sagely. Since moving to Covenly, the sisters had learned that baby goats are also called kids.

"No," Jessica said, "he means the cart he's using to wheel the box."

"Shouldn't you be in school?" Cosmo asked Jessica as he lumbered toward his garage.

"We don't have school in summer, Mr. Keene," Jessica answered, stepping out of his way.

A small card fell from Cosmo's pocket. Jessica picked it up. It read: "Finders Keepers: Used Goods and Recycling." At the bottom of the card

were written the words "Seniors' Discount" and a date: June 23.

"You dropped this, Mr. Keene," she said, hurrying after Cosmo. "By the way, what's in the box?"

He eyed her suspiciously. "No business of yours."

"You are right, Cosmo Keene," Hildegurp said, looking toward their pet emporium. "We have no business."

"No business at all," Yuckmina agreed.

Glubbifer shook her head.

"Maybe you—" Jessica began, but Cosmo shut the garage door before she could finish.

Hildegurp raised her chin.

Yuckmina tapped her toe.

Glubbifer pursed her lips.

What was Cosmo up to, anyway?

CHAPTER 3

A Real Letdown

When Jessica and the sisters arrived at the chestnut tree near the center of town, they could not believe their eyes. The town's beloved tire swing lay on the grass, its rope severed in the middle. Jessica gasped.

"Crime!" Hildegurp howled.

"Injustice!" Yuckmina yelped.

"Waah!" Glubbifer groused.

"We should investigate," Jessica said.

Hildegurp removed from her hat a long, gnarled stick with a crystal ball fixed to one end. "That's why we have the Eye, see?"

"I see," said Jessica.

"Not yet, Jessica Nibley," Yuckmina remarked. "But when the Eye shines, you will see! It shows more than things!"

"I remember," Jessica said. "Connections and clues."

Glubbifer tied the pets' leashes to the bottom of the tree. Then Hildegurp held the Eye toward the end of the hempen rope. The fibers were frayed and stuck out in all directions like a rough pom-pom. The Eye began to glow, and its pink light fell on the frayed end.

"A mystery!" cried Hildegurp.

"An enigma!" gasped Yuckmina.

"It must be a clue," said Jessica, "but what could it mean?"

Parked farther up the street was a police car.

"We should report this to Officer Nazeri," Jessica suggested.

"I agree," Hildegurp said. "But first, let us all change our hats. We must make a good impression if we want Officer Golsa Nazeri to take us seriously."

"Yes, sister," Yuckmina said. "Outfits to fit in—or is it in-fits to fit out? Oh, never mind." Yuckmina waved her wand, and immediately the sisters' hats transformed.

"Do hats matter?" Jessica objected.

"Depends on the hat," Hildegurp replied. "Try this." She tapped her wand, and Jessica shrugged under the weight of her own special hat. "There. Much better."

CHAPTER 4

New Business

Ronald Bombast, Covenly's mayor, stared from his office window, pouting. A new warehouse sat where once there was only a grassy field. The warehouse had opened in the spring—what a celebration that was! But there had been no ribbon-cutting ceremony since then. Mayor Bombast loved nothing more than cutting ribbons for news photographers. On his wall hung an assortment of ribbons—different colors, thicknesses, and textures—for any occasion. If only there *were* occasions. Poor lonely ribbons. He sighed.

Just then, Officer Nazeri, four strangely
dressed companions, and a host of animals

spilled into his office. He checked his schedule but didn't find any meeting with the constable. He sighed again.

"Oh, Officer Nazeri," the mayor cried, "what kind of mayor am I if I don't have a ribbon to cut?"

"A ribbon to cut?" Hildegurp said. "Don't be silly, Mayor Ronald Bombast. A ribbon cannot cut. You need scissors to cut."

"No, I mean—" the mayor began, but Officer Nazeri interrupted him.

"Sorry to intrude, Mr. Mayor, but someone has cut down the Covenly tire swing!"

"The swing? Down? So . . . we'd need a new one?"

"Well, yes," Officer Nazeri replied, frowning.

Mayor Bombast put his hand to his heart. "That's terrific—er, I mean, terrible news!" His eyes sparkled with life. "I want every constable on the case!"

"But, Mr. Mayor," Jessica said, "Officer Nazeri is our *only* constable."

"What? Oh yes. Crime is usually too uncommon in Covenly to require more constables. But now . . ." He looked at the group before him. Hildegurp sipped from her soda-can hat. Yuckmina, who couldn't see from under her new hat, smiled at the wall. Glubbifer shoved something furry back down under her coat. "Officer Nazeri, these are your deputies! We'll bring those vandals to justice *and* we'll have a new swing—or my name isn't Ron Bombast!"

Yuckmina held out her hand. "My name isn't Yuckmina. Pleased to not meet you." Her voice was somewhat muffled by her hat.

The mayor was too excited about his plans, and so did not shake Yuckmina's hand. "Notify the newspapers! I'll hire an artist to design a new swing! Then we'll have a ribbon cutting!"

"You mean a pair of scissors cutting," Hildegurp corrected as they shuffled out of the mayor's office.

Outside, Officer Nazeri retrieved four badges from her cruiser and pinned them onto her new deputies. "Let's solve a crime. Who would take that swing down?"

"Mr. Keene dropped a card from the recycling store," Jessica said. "Maybe he wanted to recycle the tire?"

"He *was* acting strangely," said Hildegurp.

Glubbifer nodded, sampling a sip of soda from Hildegurp's hat. Then she burped.

"What did you say?" Yuckmina asked, turning first this way, then that. "I can't hear you!"

The goat strained toward a tuft of grass growing from a sidewalk crack.

"Very well," Officer Nazeri said. "After lunch, I'll come to the pet emporium, and then we can all visit the recycling store to ask some questions. For now, do you need a lift?"

Hildegurp replied, "No, thank you, Officer Golsa Nazeri. Glubbifer is very strong. She can give us a lift."

Glubbifer demonstrated, lifting the entire group with one arm.

Officer Nazeri nodded and drove away in her cruiser. At that moment, Jessica's goat decided that *he* wanted to be at the top of the pile.

Jessica, sisters, and pets all tumbled to the ground.

CHAPTER 5

The Missing Ingredient

Chelsea Oh surveyed her kitchen counter. She had her dish. She had her recipe. She had the ingredients she needed: sunflower seeds, raisins, peanut butter, lard, and millet—plus some dried mealworms from the pet emporium. But something was missing. Chelsea tried to remember what it was.

She was distracted, however, by a commotion out near the street. She opened her door. Animals large and small burst inside. Before she knew it, she had hedgehogs in the hall, snakes in the sink, bats on the bookcase, and a goat on the

garbage can. Jessica and the sisters rushed in after them.

"Sorry, Miss Oh!" Jessica said, leaping after a spider.

Seeing all the animals jogged Chelsea's memory. "Robin!" she said.

"We are not robbing," Hildegurp protested. "We are gathering our pets."

Glubbifer separated the tongues of two frogs that had tried to catch the same fly.

"No," Chelsea clarified, "I mean the bird. Robins usually nest outside my house, but I haven't seen any this year. I was going to make a seedcake, but what's the point if there's no robin to eat it?"

"Do you have any idea why it hasn't returned?" Jessica asked.

"I did see a cat lurking about," Chelsea said.

"Did it look like . . . this?" Hildegurp pointed at Glubbifer, who held open one side of her coat to reveal Graymalkin tucked awkwardly into the lining.

"That's the cat!" Chelsea said.

"We'll find your robin for you," said Jessica, pocketing a hedgehog, "just as soon as we collect our animals."

"And we will keep Graymalkin from robbin' your robin," Hildegurp added.

Glubbifer pinched the spiders' silky leashes.
Yuckmina, still sightless under her hat, attached
a separate leash to Chelsea's mop.

"How will we do that?" Jessica asked.

From her pocket, Glubbifer withdrew the
purple flowers she had collected earlier.

"With the pansies," Hildegurp said. "We will make a potion so that Graymalkin will be kind to the robin."

"A *love* potion!" Yuckmina said. Then, tugging the mop's leash, she added, "Now let's get going, you mischief maker!"

CHAPTER 6

Undercover Sisters

"We need more than just a love potion," Jessica said when they were outside. "We have to find out who vandalized the swing, *and* we have to get Miss Oh's robin to come back to her tree. Just giving a love potion to Graymalkin won't attract the robin. We need something shiny, something tasty."

"How about shiny beads and tasty acorns?" Hildegurp said. She pointed at Yuckmina. "You, bead!" Then she pointed at Glubbifer. "You, acorn!"

Yuckmina circled the yard but soon bumped into a tree and fell, knocking off her hat. Righting herself, she reached into her hat and pulled out an assortment of glass beads. Then she put her hat back on and seemed to be deciding which direction to go.

Meanwhile, Glubbifer pulled from her pocket a possum that was munching acorns out of a paper bag. She took the bag, put the possum on her shoulder, and poured herself a handful of acorns. Then she put both bag and possum back into her pocket.

"That will attract the robin," Hildegurp said. "Now let's find the vandal." She shouted to Yuckmina, "This way! We've got detective work to do."

Yuckmina turned and walked towards Hildegurp's voice.

"If we're going to be proper detectives," Jessica said, "we should go undercover."

"I understand completely," Hildegurp said. From her hat, she produced four blankets. "We can each go under a cover."

Yuckmina walked past them and into Chelsea's shrub.

"No, I mean disguises. We need to blend in so people won't notice that we're investigating."

"Ah!" Hildegurp said. "Something ordinary?"

"Yes," Jessica agreed.

"Something average?" Hildegurp added.

"Sure," Jessica replied.

"Something plain?"

"Uh-huh," Jessica said.

Hildegurp put the blankets back into her hat and removed her wand. "I have just the thing."

Her wand crackled and sparked. In a flash,

the four of them were dressed in new outfits—
made of cardboard boxes.

"Ordinary, average, and plain," Hildegurp
said proudly.

"I can see again!" Yuckmina said.

CHAPTER 7

A Peculiar Plan

Rupert Flinch trembled outside Mayor Bombast's office. He clutched his design for the new swing. Rupert's job was selling houses, and he also liked to paint them. But he had never designed a swing before. Would the mayor like it? Was it too bold? Was it too plain?

"Oh dear, oh dear, oh dear," he said to himself.

There was only one way to find out. Rupert tugged at his collar, smoothed down the front of his shirt, and knocked.

"Come in!" the mayor yelled.

Rupert opened the door and stepped inside.

"Ah, Rupert," the mayor said, beaming. "You have your design?"

"Here, Mayor! Drawn and ready!"

The mayor took the sketch and held it up to the window.

"Oh," the mayor said thoughtfully.

Rupert wrung his hands.

"Mm-hmm."

Rupert bit his lip.

"I see. Yes! It's perfect!"

Rupert breathed a sigh of relief.

"Except . . ."

Rupert stiffened.

"It needs a ribbon."

"A ribbon?" Rupert checked his pockets. He did not have one. "Oh dear, oh dear, oh dear."

But then Rupert spotted Mayor Bombast's collection. He selected a silky red streamer and wrapped it around his drawing. "There! Now there is a ribbon on it."

Mayor Bombast frowned. "Not the drawing! I want a ribbon on the *actual* swing."

"Oh, right! I'll get to work immediately."

"Great," the mayor said. "Put it together by this afternoon!" He stuck his thumbs proudly under his suspenders. "Then I'll have a ribbon to cut!"

CHAPTER 8

How Charming

"We should return to the pet emporium," Jessica said. "Officer Nazeri will be there to meet us soon."

"And we need our love potion," Hildegurp added. "Right, Graymalkin?"

Graymalkin hissed.

Glubbifer drew her extra-long broom from her new cardboard hat. Jessica, the sisters, and all their animals piled onto the broom and zoomed back to Jitters Drive.

While Jessica put each animal back into its respective pen, jar, or place at the table, the sisters huddled over their bubbling cauldron. Glubbifer uttered a low hum while the other sisters chanted:

Little purple western flower,
Filled with sap of loving power,
Fix the heart and fix the eyes,
Make her love whom next she spies.

While Hildegurp and Yuckmina spoke, Glubbifer squeezed the pansies until purple juice dribbled out. It splashed into the broth, sending up a red mist that smelled of roses and chocolate.

"Done!" Hildegurp said, pouring the potion into a glass vial. "One drop on Graymalkin's eyes and she will love the next one she sees!"

"Let's do it now," Jessica suggested.

"We must wait until we are near the robin, Jessica Nibley," Hildegurp said. "Otherwise,

Graymalkin might love someone else instead of the bird."

"And she already loves us!" Yuckmina added. She pointed to Glubbifer, who hugged the cat.

Just then, someone knocked on the door. Jessica opened it.

"Are we ready?" Officer Nazeri asked.

Hildegurp put the potion into her pocket. "Ready," she said.

"Ready!" Yuckmina said, holding out her beads.

"Yorp!" Glubbifer said, stuffing Graymalkin back into her boxy coat.

Jessica took up her goat's leash. "I'm ready too."

"You're bringing that goat?" the constable asked.

"Can we? If we leave him, he chews things." As if proving Jessica's point, the goat nibbled at Glubbifer's cardboard shoes.

"All right, then," Officer Nazeri said.

Hildegurp, Glubbifer, and Jessica squished into the back of the police car with the pets while Yuckmina sat up front. They all put on seatbelts, except for Jessica's goat, who sat on Glubbifer's lap, and Graymalkin, who was pressed to the door. The spiders wove their own.

CHAPTER 9

Something Old, Something New

Leona Swapnik owned the thrift store, Finders Keepers. Leona loved the planet and wanted to reduce Covenly's garbage. The store accepted materials for recycling, as well as items that could be reused: clothing, books, equipment— just about anything. Leona liked to say, "If you won't keep it, let someone else find it."

But lately, the residents of Covenly had done less "finding" in her store and more "keeping" at home. If only people would donate more used things, she thought, then *more* people could take used things home.

Or was it the other way around?

As Leona puzzled over this thought, Officer Nazeri entered the store with four strangely dressed deputies. The constable introduced Jessica and the sisters.

Leona said, "Can I interest you in used shoes?"

"Actually, Leona Swapnik," Hildegurp said, "we are after sandals."

"Wonderful," Leona said. "Sandals are in aisle ten."

"She means vandals," Officer Nazeri corrected. "We're after the vandals who cut down the tire swing."

"Oh, I'm sorry," Leona groaned. "I don't sell vandals."

"Has anyone asked about recycling a tire?" Jessica inquired.

"No," Leona said, "though I would love to recycle a tire. Why, even my welcome mat is made from

recycled tires!" She pointed at the front door.

Graymalkin had slipped from Glubbifer's box-coat and dug her claws into the rubber mat. Glubbifer lifted the cat, who in turn lifted the mat. She peeled the mat away from Graymalkin's claws: *KRRIP! KRRIP! KRRIP! KRRIP!*

Leona continued, "The only customer I've had lately is Cosmo Keene. He wanted some engine parts and a sharpening stone."

"Sharpening?" Jessica repeated, frowning. "Could Mr. Keene have sharpened a knife to cut the swing's rope?" She and the sisters looked to Officer Nazeri, who pursed her lips in thought.

"He could indeed, Jessica Nibley," Hildegurp agreed.

"We will ask Cosmo Keene about this," Yuckmina added.

Just then, something caught the constable's

attention in one of the aisles. "I have an idea," she said, wandering over to examine it. She soon rejoined the group, carrying a patterned bolt of cloth.

"I'll take this fabric," she said. "It will fit in perfectly!"

"Officer Golsa Nazeri," Hildegurp said, "Let me teach you about fashion that fits in." With

a flick of her wand, their outfits changed once more. Yuckmina and Glubbifer posed. "See?"

"I mean the fabric will fit in with the environment," Officer Nazeri explained. "It looks like a wall. Criminals often return to the scene of the crime. I'll stand near the swing and pretend to be a wall. Then, when the vandals return, I'll catch them!"

Looking Up

Cosmo Keene raised his garage door. Sunlight glinted off the glossy red paint and shiny chrome engine of his new lawn mower. He wheeled it outside just as Officer Nazeri's cruiser pulled up to the curb. Jessica Nibley and those weird sisters tumbled out of the car, followed by a goat.

Officer Nazeri drove away.

The goat nibbled at the grass.

Cosmo scowled.

"Remove that goat!" he said. "I'll cut the grass myself." He had once had a scary encounter with Jessica's goat.

"That's a nice mower," Jessica remarked.

He straightened. "It's souped up."

"Lawn mower soup?" Yuckmina said. Glubbifer grimaced.

"I mean I made it more powerful," Cosmo said, "so the job would be easier."

"It's easiest if it pushes itself," Yuckmina suggested. "Do you agree, Glubbifer?"

Glubbifer nodded, then zapped her wand. The mower quivered.

"Cosmo Keene," Hildegurp interrupted, "did you cut the tire swing rope?"

He leaned on the mower's handle and smiled at the sky. "What a wonderful idea," he said. "No more noise from troublemaking kids in the park! But no, I haven't cut anything."

"But you bought a sharpening stone from Leona Swapnik," Yuckmina said.

"Yes," he said, "for the—"

"Look!" Jessica cut in, pointing. "What's that under the eave?"

Hildegurp looked to the sky. "It is not eve, Jessica Nibley. It is day." She held out her wrist to show Jessica the time.

"An eave is the overhanging edge of a roof," Jessica said. "Look!"

A wad of mud, twigs, and fibers sat snugly between the wall and the downspout.

Yuckmina removed the Eye and held it up. Pink light streamed out of it and made the fibers in the mud glow.

"We must get closer," Hildegurp said. She yanked her broom from her hat.

Cosmo immediately backed away. "Oh no," he said, waving his hands. "Not that again." He had also had a scary encounter with the sisters' broom.

Out of respect for Cosmo, Hildegurp put it back into her hat. Instead, she climbed onto Glubbifer's shoulders. Yuckmina climbed onto Hildegurp's shoulders. Jessica climbed onto Yuckmina's shoulders and peered at the muddy splotch.

Jessica gasped. "It's a nest!" she said. "With a bird and three blue eggs!"

At the word "bird," Graymalkin peered from Glubbifer's coat with considerable interest.

"Blue eggs?" repeated Hildegurp. "We must cheer them up! Come, sisters! A song!"

"I mean the eggs are *colored* blue," Jessica clarified. "Robin's eggs. This must be the robin

Miss Oh asked us about. Hildegurp, get your love potion ready!"

As Hildegurp rooted through her pockets, Graymalkin crawled out from Glubbifer's coat and climbed up the sisters toward the nest. Jessica's goat decided to climb as well, hopping onto Glubbifer's shoulders, then Hildegurp's, then Yuckmina's, then Jessica's. Cosmo, meanwhile, put on his earmuffs, getting ready to cut the grass.

Things were about to get messy.

CHAPTER 11

Falling Down

Glubbifer held three people, a cat, and a goat upon her shoulders. They were like a tower with too small a base. Graymalkin strained toward the nest.

She didn't quite reach.

Hildegurp pulled the potion from her pocket. Graymalkin's claws pulled on Jessica's sleeve. Cosmo pulled the rip cord of his souped-up lawn mower. Yuckmina pulled a muscle.

"Ow!" cried Jessica.

"Ow!" howled Yuckmina.

"Meow!" meowed Graymalkin.

Cosmo's engine roared to life. Startled, the robin bolted from its nest. Graymalkin leapt after it, unbalancing Jessica, who unbalanced Yuckmina, who unbalanced Hildegurp. For the second time that day, they fell into a heap.

Glubbifer's wand stuck out from her pocket and the goat snatched it, thinking it was something to chew.

Graymalkin chased the robin, then pounced, landing on the lawn mower's engine.

As the goat lifted the wand, a stream of sparks shot toward the rumbling mower, causing it to lurch forward.

"Uh-oh," Jessica said.

CHAPTER 12

A Grand Display

Mayor Bombast waited beneath the chestnut tree checking his watch. It was time to dedicate the new swing. Rupert, Leona, the news reporters, the city officials, the spectators— everyone was there. Someone had even erected a new wall for the occasion.

"But where's Officer Nazeri?" the mayor asked.

Rupert shrugged.

"Well, we can't wait forever," he said. He held up the small mirror he always kept in his pocket. He checked his hair, his teeth, his nostrils.

"Looking good, Ron!" he said to himself. He held his scissors ready.

Then he checked the swing.

It was the *same* swing. Rupert had simply tied the two ends of rope together.

The mayor glared.

Rupert gulped. "Oh dear, oh dear, oh dear," he said. "You asked me to put it all together. Here it is—all put together!"

"Fine," the mayor growled. "But there's no ribbon!"

Rupert pointed to a small bow painted onto the tire. "You said you wanted it on the *actual* swing."

"I meant a ribbon I can cut!" the mayor barked. "Fortunately, I keep extras for emergencies." He withdrew a long red ribbon from his pocket and strung it across the swing. Then he snipped it in half with the scissors.

Cameras flashed and the spectators cheered.

"I want a group photo too" the mayor said to a reporter. "Maybe against this wall?"

But a gathering noise up the street had grabbed the reporter's attention. A strange sound carried on the wind—a sound like a tweeting, thundering yowl.

Officer Nazeri jumped past Mayor Bombast. "Vandals!" she yelled.

"Where did she come from?" the mayor wondered. "And what happened to that new wall?"

CHAPTER 13

Fuss and Feathers

The robin flew for its life.

The mower screamed after the little bird, tearing across lawns and boulevards, through shrubs and flower beds, across streets and

driveways, over tree roots and curbs. Graymalkin clung desperately to the engine.

"After that mower!" Hildegurp said.

"And that meower!" Yuckmina added. They chased Graymalkin with their love potion.

Jessica's goat ran for his life.

Glubbifer and Jessica chased him, hoping

to snatch the sparking wand from his mouth. Every time he zigged and zagged, jumped and turned, spun and darted, the lawn mower moved the exact same way.

Cosmo chased his mower. The cat was a terrible lawn cutter. "If you want a job done right," he huffed, "never leave it to a cat!"

Meanwhile, Officer Nazeri ran behind Cosmo. She blew her whistle and shouted, "Stop, vandal!"

Cosmo was not a vandal, so he did not stop.

Chelsea Oh jumped for her life.

She had been gathering nuts and seeds for her recipe when her beloved robin whooshed by. Then a cat on a mower rocketed past and snatched her recipe.

"Hey!" Chelsea cried. "My recipe!"

She did not see Hildegurp and Yuckmina running toward her.

Rupert Flinch felt like he was living a charmed
life.

He'd successfully completed his swing
project—quite an accomplishment! Still, he

wanted someone special with whom to share
this joy. He looked up. Chelsea Oh faced him,
shouting something and waving.

He smiled and waved back.

Mayor Bombast was having the time of his life.

The new swing was complete, he'd cut a ribbon, and the reporters were ready to photograph him. All he needed was a baby to kiss. Voters liked nice people, and mayors who kissed babies looked nice.

One mother held her baby out to him.

"Hello, little one," the mayor said. "Would you like a photo with Ron Bombast?"

"Blech," the baby said.

"Great!" Mayor Bombast beamed. He lifted the baby and puckered his lips.

He did not get to kiss the baby.

CHAPTER 14

All Together Now

The robin sailed up into the chestnut tree, while below several things happened at once.

First, the mower slammed into the tree, launching Graymalkin through the air. She knocked the baby from Mayor Bombast's arms just as the cameras flashed. Mayor Bombast kissed Graymalkin instead. Officer Nazeri caught the baby.

At the same time, the goat rammed into Rupert. Rupert fell over, and the goat fell on top of him.

Meanwhile, Hildegurp and Yuckmina crashed into Chelsea. Hildegurp's love potion flew from her hands and splashed into Chelsea's eyes.

Rupert sat up with the goat still on top of him.

Hildegurp shrieked, "Oh, Rupert Flinch! How you are changed!"

Then the goat spied the mower's grass catcher, which was full of grass. He climbed down off Rupert, dropped the wand, and munched on the grass.

That's when Chelsea sat up, wobbling a little, and blinked. She caught sight of Rupert.

Her eyes twinkled.

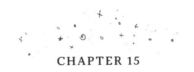

CHAPTER 15

Mystery Solved

On the tree branch, a second robin joined the first. Its red feathers were richer than those of the first robin.

"Is everyone all right?" Jessica called.

Officer Nazeri handed the baby to its relieved mother.

Mayor Bombast handed Graymalkin to Glubbifer, who was also relieved.

Leona Swapnik handed Cosmo his broken lawn mower. Cosmo was not relieved.

"Not so fast, Cosmo," said Officer Nazeri, taking out her handcuffs. "Or should I say *vandal*?!"

"What?" said Cosmo.

"Wait!" Jessica cried. "Mr. Keene is innocent, Officer Nazeri."

The sisters gasped and turned to Jessica for an explanation.

"Mr. Keene didn't cut the rope. When we investigated, we noticed that the rope was frayed. But look at this cut ribbon with its straight edge. If the rope had been cut, the fibers would have stayed twisted together."

"Then why buy a sharpening stone?" Officer Nazeri asked Cosmo.

"For my lawn mower blade!" he answered.

"The rope was frayed because the robins pulled threads from it," Jessica continued. "After the new warehouse was built on the field, the robins had no long grasses anymore. Instead, the male plucked hemp fibers from the swing's rope, and the female used them to build the nest."

"So the robins vandalized the swing?" Officer Nazeri concluded. "Then I must arrest those birds." She held out her handcuffs.

"But they only made a home for their eggs to be safe," Jessica explained.

"A hempen home!" Yuckmina marveled.

Officer Nazeri paused. "Safety is good," she said, eyeing the female robin. "You are a responsible mom." She held out her finger, and the male robin flew to it. "And you're a pretty good fellow, yourself." She put her cuffs away.

Jessica said, "The rope got thinner and thinner until it snapped. Cosmo wasn't planning to recycle the tire. He went to Finders Keepers to treat himself to new lawn mower parts because . . . well, do you want to tell them, Mr. Keene?"

Cosmo sighed over his broken lawn mower. "It's my birthday," he muttered.

Jessica added, "We noticed the date on his seniors' discount card: June 23. That's today!"

"Why didn't you tell anyone?" Leona asked. "We could have thrown you a party."

"Parties are noisy," Cosmo grumbled. "And I don't like noise!"

CHAPTER 16

Tying Up Loose Ends

"**Y**ou can have a quiet birthday if you want," Hildegurp said. "We like quiet, right, Glubbifer?"

Glubbifer gave a thumbs-up.

Yuckmina removed an elaborate birthday cake from her hat. "How about this?"

"Cake?" said Chelsea. "Right! I nearly forgot! I have a seedcake almost ready for the robin. I just need some nuts to complete the recipe and something shiny to decorate the plate."

Yuckmina held out her beads. Glubbifer cracked the acorns between her knuckles, then offered Chelsea the crumbs.

"Perfect!" Chelsea said. "Maybe *you'd* like to help me, Rupert?"

"Sure," he replied. "I'll also paint the robins' new house."

"Paint mud?" the mayor scoffed.

"I mean a *painting* of the robin's house. I feel responsible for selling their field for the warehouse. Perhaps I could make up for it by planting more grasses and trees."

"We'll all help with that, Mr. Flinch," Jessica said. "Will the town let us plant on some land, Mr. Mayor?"

The mayor conferred with his officials, then nodded.

"I'll watch for noise violations so that Cosmo can have a quiet party," Officer Nazeri added.

"And I," Mayor Bombast announced, taking another ribbon from his pocket, "will cut this ribbon for the photographers!"

"I'll provide spare parts for Cosmo's mower!" said Leona Swapnik. "By the way," she said to Hildegurp, "your outfits are really something!"

"They are?" Hildegurp said, frowning. "We were trying to fit in."

"Fitting in is just being comfortable with your own choices," Leona said. "If you ever want to donate your used clothing, I'm always looking for unique items. One person's trash is another's treasure!"

"Unique, yes," Hildegurp repeated, nodding.

"What about the swing?" Rupert interjected. "I've tied the rope back together, but now it's too high for children to swing on."

Glubbifer reached up and untied the top knot, then found a lower branch. When she had finished tying it again, the swing was just the right height.

"We still have one problem," Jessica said. "Our love potion is used up, but we haven't brought the robin back to Miss Oh's tree."

Chelsea held her hands up in caution. "Let's leave the nest where it is," she said. "If we touch it, the robins may abandon the eggs."

"Oh fine," Cosmo grumbled. "As long as they aren't too loud."

"But Graymalkin may still bother the robins," Jessica mused. "If only there were a way to keep the birds safe from her. Something like ... a bell?"

Glubbifer placed Graymalkin on the ground, then removed a large bell from her hat. She placed the bell over the cat.

"I meant *collar* bell," Jessica clarified.

"Call her Belle?" Hildegurp repeated. "Instead of Graymalkin? Okay. Here, Belle!"

"Belle can't hear under *that*," Yuckmina said, pointing.

"No," Jessica said. "I mean let's put a tiny bell on the collar around her neck."

Glubbifer exchanged the large bell for a smaller one. She attached it to Graymalkin's collar. Graymalkin jingled as she walked.

Officer Nazeri cupped her hand and whispered into Mayor Bombast's ear.

"Really?" he said. "A photo too?"

Officer Nazeri nodded.

The mayor cleared his throat. "For her dedication to protecting robins, I wish to present our first Covenly Ecojustice Award to . . . Jessica Nibley!"

Mayor Bombast then expertly fashioned a ribbon into a flower, which he pinned to Jessica's rat costume in time for another photo.

Jessica bit her lip. "Umm, thank you, Mayor Bombast, but this award should be shared. The sisters provided the bell, Miss Oh is providing a seedcake, Mr. Flinch is going to plant more grasses and trees—"

"Yes!" Chelsea agreed. "Isn't Rupert wonderful?"

Jessica continued, "Mr. Keene is providing shelter for the robins' nest. And even you, Mayor Bombast, have helped by providing city land for planting."

"So I have!" Mayor Bombast agreed. "This calls for another picture!"

The group gathered again. Somehow Jessica's flower ended up on Mayor Bombast's lapel.

The sisters set up a table and chairs on the lawn. Chelsea placed the seedcake near the tree. Everyone sat quietly to eat their cake, whispering "Happy birthday" to Cosmo, who mumbled "Thank you" between bites.

Seedcake for Robins

Ingredients

2½ cups (625 mL) shelled sunflower seeds or acorns

1½ cups (375 mL) uncooked millet, barley, or quinoa

1 cup (250 mL) raisins or dried cranberries

¼ cup (60 mL) dried mealworms from a pet emporium (optional)

½ lb. (225 g) lard

1 cup (250 mL) crunchy peanut butter

What to do

1. In a bowl, mix seeds, grain, fruit, and worms.

2. In a saucepan, melt lard and peanut butter together over low heat, stirring occasionally.

3. To the seed mixture, add the melted peanut butter and lard. Stir until blended.

4. Pour the mixture into a loaf pan. Place the loaf pan in the freezer for 2 hours. As it chills, it will become firm.

5. When the seedcake has hardened, remove it from the loaf pan and get an adult's help to cut it into individual cakes, about as large as a slice of bread.

6. Place cut seedcakes in individual suet cages to hang outside, or on paper plates to put on the ground. (Robins usually look for food at ground level.) Caution: seedcakes on the ground may also attract squirrels!

Keep leftovers in the fridge.

Mark David Smith has never had sisters, but he does have two cats—neither of whom is very good at mowing the lawn. And though he has never cast a spell, he does find life with his wife and children pretty magical. Mark is also the author of the picture book *The Deepest Dig*. He lives in Port Coquitlam, British Columbia.

Kari Rust loves the "magic" that
happens when an illustration comes to
life. She conjures art in an old house in
Vancouver, British Columbia, where she
lives with her husband and two kids. She
sees many birds in their big, twisted birch
tree. The robin, however, remains elusive.
Kari is the author and illustrator of *Tricky*
and *The House at the End of the Road*.

Coming Soon
Book three in the Weird Sisters series!

The town of Covenly's fall fair is in full swing, and when a prized show chicken goes missing, Jessica and the Weird Sisters—Hildegurp, Yuckmina, and Glubbifer—have a new mystery to solve. Suspecting *fowl* play, the four friends team up to find the hapless hen in a madcap hunt that involves an enchanted roller coaster, a frog in a top hat, and a sticky trail of goo. Will they find the fall fair's fowl? Find out in this third charming and hilarious Weird Sisters mystery.